Jim and Jam
and the Band

this is
Jim

in every picture
look for his pet mouse
Jam

Written and devised by Angela Littler
Illustrated by Anita McEwen

HODDER AND STOUGHTON
LONDON   SYDNEY   AUCKLAND   TORONTO

Jim and Jam
go to the park.
Jim wants
to hear the band.

☆ Can you follow the path to the bandstand?
Trace it with your finger.

- Do you think all the people on the path are going to the bandstand?
- Count the ducks. Which one is different?

Here is Jim's friend, Polly
and her dog, Pip.
Jim waves to them.
They can hear the band together.

☆ Can you find two seats together
for Jim and Polly?

- How many people are reading newspapers?
- Can you point to the biggest newspaper?

The band plays.

Jim and Polly listen.

They like the music.

Pip likes the flowerbed better.

☆ Find these instruments
in the band:

cymbals

tuba

clarin

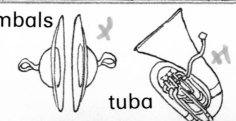

drum

French horn

flute

trumpet

trombone

It is windy now.

Look!

Polly loses her red balloon.

Jim is cross with Pip.

☆ Spot the differences between
the bandsmen's uniforms.

- Pretend to play some of the instruments.
- Ask someone to guess what you are playing.

The hats blow away.
The papers blow away.
Jim and Polly chase them.
Pip helps.

 Five bandsmen have lost their hats. Can you
find them? Can you see three other hats, too?

- Count the hats in the tree.
- Can you see Polly's red balloon?

The children pick up
the hats and papers.
They carry them
back to the bandstand.

☆ Help Jim and Polly find their way through
the flowerbeds and back to the bandstand.

• Follow the path with your finger.

Everybody says thank you.
Jim and Polly
are happy to help.
Jim plays the tuba
just for fun.

☆ Can you find the right hat for
each bandsman?

- What colour are the hat badges?
- Where is the bandleader's hat?
- Who is cross? Why?

It is late.
Time to go home.
Goodbye, Jim!
Goodbye, Jam!

☆ Can you see some tall bandsmen?
How many?

- Are people waving with their left or right hands?
- Count the short bandsmen.

Word and Picture Puzzle

hat

tree

drum

dog

newspaper

trumpet

balloon

chair

tuba

bandstand

duck

cymbals

Look at these pictures and read the words several times.
Try putting a strip of paper (or a coin, or your hand)
over the pictures. Now can you read what each word says?

Hats Off!

Here is a game to make and play with your friends. Find an empty cereal box and paint it or cover it with wallpaper, using children's glue. Stand it on one long side, and stick four cardboard tubes on the top. They can be long or short. Make faces on the tubes with stick-on shapes or coloured pens. Now make a hat for each face with a cotton ball. Decorate the hats with feathers, flowers, sequins or glitter. Pop the hats lightly on top of each face. Give each player a jumbo straw. Now you are ready to play: each player has four goes to try and blow the hats off the faces with the straw. The one who blows off most hats, wins. If it is a draw, then have another go to see who can blow the hats farthest away, and win.

Make a Tooter

Use a long cardboard tube (a short one will not work so well) and make two or three air-holes in the middle of the tube with a sharp pencil. Tear off a piece of new, smooth kitchen foil and fit it tightly over one end of the tube with a rubber band. Now 'toot' down your tube and you will make a loud trumpet sound. To keep the sound sharp, replace the foil when it gets crumpled, and make sure the air-holes are clear.

Make Shakers

Put 3 or 4 teaspoons of dried peas or lentils into an empty yoghurt pot, and cover the top with foil, held by a rubber band. Now you have a good shaker to shake in time with your favourite songs. You can make another kind of shaker by putting peas or lentils into a clean, empty washing-up liquid bottle. Replace the cap – and shake away! (If you do not have a funnel to help get the peas into the bottle, use a rolled-up triangle of paper).

Make Scrapers

Find two empty boxes about the same size. Individual-sized cereal boxes are good, or use large, empty matchboxes. With children's glue, stick a piece of sandpaper onto one side of each box (coarse glasspaper is best, if you have it). When the glue is dry, you can scrape the boxes against each other in time with your favourite songs or poems.

Musical Bingo

A game for two to four players. For each instrument, cut out 5 little squares of paper and draw a picture of the instrument on each. Use the pictures below as a guide. Number each picture clearly from 1 to 5. Put all the paper squares into a hat, and jumble them up. Each player decides what instrument s/he wants to be.

One player is also the caller, who picks one paper at a time out of the hat, calling out what is on it – for example, "Drum, three". The person who is 'Drum' takes the paper and puts it on square number 3 of the drum column. The first player to fill up all 5 spaces is the winner. Play on until everyone has finished.

flute

drum

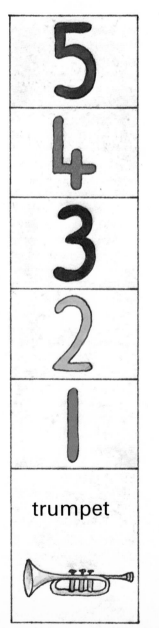

trumpet

tuba